Cathy Hopkins

Tony & Lucy

Mates, Dates

An episode from

The Secret Story

www. Free in exchange for a •£1.00 WBD Book Token
•or €1.50 in Ireland

WORLD
BOOK
DAY
worldbookday.com

Flip over for another fun book   £1

Cathy Hopkins

Mates, Dates

An episode from

The Secret Story

This book has been specially written and published for World Book Day 2009. World Book Day is a worldwide celebration of books and reading, and was marked in over 30 countries around the globe last year. For further information please see www.worldbookday.com World Book Day in the UK and Ireland is made possible by generous sponsorship from National Book Tokens, participating publishers, authors and booksellers. Booksellers who accept the £1 World Book Day Token kindly agree to bear the full cost of redeeming it.

Piccadilly Press • London

First published in Great Britain in 2009
by Piccadilly Press Ltd,
5 Castle Road, London NW1 8PR

A catalogue record for this book is available from
the British Library.

ISBN 13: 978 0 9559446 42

1 3 5 7 9 10 8 6 4 2

Cover design by Simon Davis

Lucy

It was a moment that was to change my life forever.

I was sitting in the passenger seat, staring out of the window as Dad drove us home. It was raining – which seemed fitting for the grey mood I was in.

'How was school?' asked Dad.

I shrugged my shoulders. 'OK,' I replied. I didn't feel like talking. I was thinking about Izzie. She's been my best mate since junior school but something weird has been going on lately. A new girl arrived at the end of the summer term. Nesta Williams. She created quite a stir. She's stunning for one thing – tall, dark-skinned with black hair like silk down her back, and she's so confident. She's everything I'm not. I'm small, blonde and totally unsure of who I am or where I fit in.

This September, we went into Year Nine and

Izzie started hanging out with Nesta and now she's always like, Nesta said this, Nesta did that. I'm scared that Izzie feels that she's outgrown me, like I'm boring compared to her new glam mate. Or too childish.

The other night, we tried to get into a fifteen movie and we were turned away. I knew it was my fault because Izzie and Nesta both look sixteen. I couldn't kid myself otherwise, thanks to Josie who is a mean girl from our school and was there in the queue. She looked my way then called out for everyone to hear, 'Anyone can see the midget's underage,' and when she swanned into the movie with a bunch of Year Elevens, she said, 'Leave the children to play'. That hurt. And Nesta looked cross – probably because we hadn't got in and it was because of me. I think she felt embarrassed to be seen with me too. So . . . I'm not sure if there's going to be room for me in Izzie's life anymore. She clearly wants to move on and hang with the more grown-up cool crowd.

Dad slowed down the car as the traffic lights changed and it was then that I saw him. A vision of boy babeness. He was coming out of the school gates at St Michael's and he crossed the road in front of us. Dark. Handsome. Chiselled jaw. A Disney prince in a schoolboy's black and white uniform, alive and walking the streets of North London. My heart sped up. It really did – *boom banga bang* in my chest – and I felt my stomach twist as I watched him. He didn't see me. He was talking to another boy. They were laughing about something.

Ohmigod, I thought. *After all these months of looking for a boy and only finding weedy wombats. There he is.*

'Lucy, you're blushing,' said Izzie later that same day.

'No, I'm not,' I objected, although I felt colour flush to my cheeks. Izzie is lucky, she never blushes. She has the looks of a typical Irish colleen: dark hair, green eyes, pale skin. Pale skin that always looks cool and in control.

I hate that I blush, I thought. *It always gives my secrets away. I bet Nesta never blushes.* I've tried wearing pale make-up to hide my red cheeks but it doesn't work – nothing does and my embarrassment is always evident to anyone who happens to be looking at me.

Izzie raised an eyebrow and gave me a look as if to say, 'Pull the other one'. I turned away from her and the computer where we'd been checking our horoscopes. I'd gone straight round to her house as soon as I'd had supper.

'So. What's going on?' asked Izzie.

There was no point in hiding it. I could never keep anything from her for long and I was bursting to tell her my news. 'I'm in love,' I blurted.

'Brilliant,' said Izzie. 'Who's the lucky boy?'

I shrugged my shoulders. 'Don't know.'

'What do you mean, you don't know?'

'I haven't actually spoken to him yet.'

'Ah. Do you know his name?'

I shook my head. 'I know what school he goes to. St Michael's.'

Izzie smiled. 'I suppose that's a start. And, er . . . how do you know it's love?'

'I just do,' I replied. I did.

'OK,' said Izzie. 'You just do.'

I nodded and settled back on the beanbag on the floor of her bedroom. I felt so much better. It was me and Iz doing our horoscopes and chatting like we always did. And I had seen the perfect boy. 'Yeah. I've never felt like this before and I just know he's going to feel the same when we meet. Er . . . don't tell anyone though, will you?'

'Course not,' said Izzie. 'Not if you don't want. Your secret is safe with me.'

Tony

'So come on, Tony. Tell us your secret,' begged Robin as we crossed the road outside school. 'I *need* help.'

'No secret,' I said. When we reached the other side, I saw that Annabelle Wilson and her mate Mira Jones were coming towards us on the pavement.

As soon as she spotted us, Mira flicked blond hair back off her face. 'Hi, Tone,' she said in a low voice and gave me a flirty look.

'Hi, girls,' I replied, and gave her a flirty look back (eye contact held a second too long, slightly raised eyebrow and slow smile) then I did the same to Annabelle. She blushed pink. I'd dated both of them last year. Not at the same time. I'd never have got away with it seeing as they're mates. Mira in the winter for six weeks, (a record for me as my cut off is usually around four) and

Annabelle in the spring for just a few dates. She was sweet but boring after a while. I like a girl who can hold her own in the conversation stakes. Mira was more interesting but she got possessive and I don't do clingy as she found out after yet another 'And where have you been and who with?' conversations.

The girls walked past and Rob and I continued on our way up towards Highgate. Rob turned around.

'They're watching,' he said.

I shrugged and carried on walking. 'Rule number one, my friend, never turn around. Makes you look too keen.'

'Oh right,' said Rob. 'I forgot. Treat 'em mean to keep 'em keen.'

'Ish,' I said. 'You don't have to be mean, just don't look desperate. Girls always want what they can't have. Remember that.'

Rob did a mock salute. 'So come on, Tony, spill. You clearly have the ability to pull any girl you want and I need a few hints.'

'Don't try too hard. Don't do needy.' I didn't know what else to tell him. I've never had to try.

Girls like me. Always have, but I don't think it's because of anything I say or don't say, do or don't do. Sometimes I joke around and say I am the Master when it comes to girls but I'm not totally serious. It's simple. I like girls, they like me. Lucky me.

When we got up to Highgate, we went into Costa. We go in most nights after school and always try to bag the stools by the window. That way, we can check out the babes on the street as well as watch the ones inside.

Robin went to get our drinks while I got our places. He's been my mate since I changed schools at the end of last year. Like mine, his family had just moved to the area so he was a newbie too. He's a good guy. On the level. Nice-looking boy, Robin, but no real talent when it comes to pulling. He's always, like hey, I've got this real cool chat up line, want to hear it? And I'd go, Robin, reality check, man. You don't need a chat up line to get on with girls, you just talk to them like you like them, like you're interested in what they have to say. Works every time.

Now he's reckons he's in love. Hannah is her

name. I've never seen him like this over a girl before. He only met her last week when we went bowling. She's OK. Not my type. Bit tomboyish – figure like a boy's too, straight up and down, and she doesn't seem to make much effort with her clothes, she's always in jeans and an old T-shirt. I like girls to look like girls. Especially those with a bit of style about them.

At that moment, Sienna Jeffrey waved from across the street. I waved back. She giggled and headed for the bus stop. About two minutes later, my phone bleeped that I had a text. It was from Sienna. *Wot R U doing Fri pm? XXX*

Rob came back with our cappuccinos and read the text over my shoulder. He sighed. 'Sienna again? Isn't that the hundredth text this week?'

I nodded. 'Might have to change my phone.'

'Just text her back and say, there's a queue and you're way down the line.'

I laughed but I could never be that cruel. Girls have feelings and it's hard letting them down sometimes. We had a snog at a party a few weeks ago and now she thinks that we're an item. But

Rob is right. There is a queue. My mobile bleeped that I had another text. This time it was Carrie Johnson. *I know you feel the same way as I do,* she'd written. *'Fraid not,* I thought as I pressed delete, then glanced up to see that Jess Macdonald and Charlotte Rosin were on their way over. Rob perked up immediately as they are two total Barbie babes.

'Don't look so keen, look cool,' I whispered to Rob.

'Aye, aye, Captain,' he said and assumed a bored look and turned to look out the window.

Atta boy, Rob, I thought, *you'll get there in the end.*

Lucy

'I do *not* believe you did that! How could you?'

'I'm sorry, Luce,' said Izzie as we went into assembly on Monday morning. 'It just slipped out.'

I was mad. *Really* mad. Izzie had told Nesta my private business about being in love. 'It was *meant* to be a secret,' I said.

'I know. I know but we were talking about boys and love and stuff on the phone last night and it just came out.'

Grrrrr, I thought. *GrrrRRRRRRRR.* I wasn't sure if I was more mad that she'd told Nesta my secret or because she'd been having a laugh with her about boys. Having a laugh and chatting about boys was what I did with Izzie. Iz and me. *Me* and Iz. The two of us. *Two.* It was another example of how things were changing with our friendship and I wasn't sure I liked it.

'I don't want her coming with us on our "Find the Mystery Contestant" outings,' I said. We'd agreed two things at the weekend. One was that we were going to refer to the boy as the MC, the Mystery Contestant, and the other was that I needed a plan to meet him. Izzie had suggested that we go up to Highgate and hang out after school every night. It was a good plan. A great plan and I felt excited about it. I could see it in my mind's eye. I'd spot him. He'd see me. He'd feel the connection just like I had when he crossed the road in front of me. Everything would go into slow motion. Sadly the image in my mind's eye kept getting poked out by Nesta. What if he saw her first? I wouldn't stand a chance. She's a boy magnet. She could be a model if she wanted. I'm not even near her league.

'No worries,' said Izzie. 'Nesta's got rehearsals for the school show just about every night.'

'Does she know about the plan?' I asked.

Izzie looked sheepish.

'Izzie!'

Izzie threw up her hands. 'Give her a break, Lucy. She was really pleased you'd seen a boy you liked. And OK, so she knows the plan but she's not going to ruin it for you. She won't be coming with us. She wants to be friends, you know.'

'She wants to be friends with *you*,' I said and then I hated myself for acting like a strop queen. I don't know what's the matter with me lately. Jealous. Moody. Cross! And that can all be in the space of five minutes some days. Not only that, our teacher Wacko Watkins has given us a project – *What Makes Me Me?* It feels like the final straw. Seems everyone in our class has done it no problemo. They all know what they want to do when they leave school, what they're about, what their goals are. Not me though. I don't know who I am, what I want to be or where I fit. The one thing I have ever been sure of in my life was that Izzie Foster was my best friend and now even that isn't a definite any more.

Lucy's diary
Friday

Quelle week *terrible* (to be read in a French accent). Actually, if anyone does read this, I will have to kill them (that's YOU Lal). Note to self – remember to

13

always lock my diary away after I've written in it, especially after the humungous secret I am about to write in here. Also change the hiding place from under my mattress because I think Lal may have cottoned on to where I've been keeping it and we all know how nosy he is. Luckily I haven't written too much in it so far, but, now that Izzie isn't as available, I probably will. So. Lal, if you ever find my new hiding place and read it again, you are a dead man and I mean that.

What a week! After three evenings up in Highgate with Izzie, looking for my mystery boy in the cafés, at the bus stops, at the school gates, we were beginning to think that maybe I had dreamt him. We saw boys of every shape and size, but did the MC appear? Not on your nelly, as my gran used to say.

And then . . .

This evening, after checking out the school gates, we headed up to Costa and that's where my life, my dreams, my future were shattered for ever. Just before we got to the café, Nesta appeared. My heart sank because I could see that every boy in the vicinity was checking her out. I thought it was game over for me. If mystery boy saw her, he'd fall in love, think that I was her pet elf (although

14

I think I have grown a quarter of an inch and am now four foot ten and a half!) and that would be it, end of story.

Just as we were about to go into Costa, Nesta took a detour into the newsagents. Iz and I went to get drinks and scanned the café. So far so good – no sign of my boy.

I looked out of the window in case he was on the street. Suddenly my mouth dropped open. Nesta was coming out of the newsagent. And she wasn't alone. She was with him! *HIM*! My MC!

I could hardly believe my eyes. Iz and I had spent almost a whole week looking for him and, not only had Nesta bumped into him, but in two minutes, two minutes, she'd got chatting to him! Talk about a fast worker, I thought.

Seconds later, Nesta and his lovely lovelinesss were standing before me. (He was even better looking close up.) And then Nesta introduced him as her brother, Tony! Brother!!!? I swear my jaw must have hit the floor. It didn't add up. Nesta is dark-skinned. Tony is white. (I was a colour all of my own. Red, red, red.) Turns out he's Nesta's half brother. Same dad, different mum. Nesta's mum is her dad's second wife. But MY MC IS NESTA'S BROTHER!!!!!!! Ugabugabulah!

15

And that's when I knew that I could never tell anyone, – not Izzie, certainly not Nesta – that Tony was the boy I'd been looking for all week. If he ever found out that I'd been up there looking for him, he'd think I was totally desperate. And if Iz and Nesta found out, it would be a huge laugh for them but utterly humiliating for me.

And then things got even worse – so bad, that I think the tiniest detail of our conversation will be imprinted on my brain for ever. My mind has been replaying and replaying the scene over and over in the fear that I may have given my secret away.

'So. Which one of you is Lucy?' Tony asked.

'I am,' I whispered. I felt wobbly and faint.

'Nesta tells me that you've got your eye on one of the St Michael's boys. (*Hah! Like, yeah. Like, I have and it's you. Argh!*) I go there, so I might know him. (*Hahahaha. Not. More like double argh!*) I'm in Year Twelve. What year is he in? What does he look like?' (*What does he look like? You. Argh. Oh! My! God! This is like my worse nightmare. It can't be happening.*)

My cheeks burned furiously. I remember I stuttered something stupid like, 'Er, tall, er . . . hair. He was, um, too far away for me to get a close look.'

And then Izzie piped up: 'Just find us the best-looking boy at your school and that will be him.' (By this time, I think I might have left my body and have been watching the whole scene from the ceiling.)

Tony flashed me a cheeky smile. 'Best-looking boy in the school? But . . . you're looking at him.'

I may have laughed a little too hysterically at this point. Best-looking boy in the school? *I know you are – but do you know I know? Argh. Argh. Argh.*

I couldn't wait to get out of there. What a total awful outcome, the worse possible. What with Tony asking me to describe the boy and Nesta saying that she reckoned that the reason I hadn't seen the boy was because he might have been doing some extra curriculum class like Tony often did (!!!!), I could not believe that they hadn't twigged that Tony was the One. It was soooo obvious to me. But it appeared that they hadn't. And now I can never tell Izzie or Nesta and especially not him or he will think I am a sad weirdo. It will have to be my secret forever.

Tony

'So what do you think of Lucy and Izzie?' asked Nesta when we got on the bus to go home.

'Sweet,' I told her.

'Both of them?'

'Which is which again?'

'Lucy is the blonde one.'

'Yeah. She's a sweet kid. I liked the way she blushed. I like girls who blush. It's cute.'

'Izzie is the taller one. She's got beautiful eyes, hasn't she?'

I laughed. 'Has she now? Can't say I noticed. Nesta, don't even start. Your mates are way too young for me.' Nesta had done this before – when we lived down in Bristol. She was always bringing her friends home from her school who then got a crush on me and she'd get mad at me if I didn't fancy them.

18

'I wasn't starting anything like that, you dope-head. In fact, if you showed any interest in either Izzie or Lucy, I'd have to kill you. I know what you're like and I don't want to be held responsible for romantic let-downs.'

'No chance, Nesta. Way too young for me. I like girls with a bit of experience.'

'Good because I want them to like me and I don't want you messing things up by playing with their heads or their hearts.'

'As if. But what do you mean you want them to like you? They're your mates, aren't they? They have to like you. That's the rules. Mates like you.'

'They're *new* mates,' said Nesta. 'Still early days and I'm not sure that Lucy likes me at all. I think Izzie does but Lucy can be a bit aloof some days and I don't know what's going on in her head.'

'She's the blonde one, yeah?'

Nesta nodded. 'Yeah. Like, I've been round her house and met her family, she's got two brothers and we all had a laugh, but then some-times she goes quiet and I catch her looking at me and . . . I don't know what's she's thinking.'

Tony squeezed my arm. 'Been tough for you,

hasn't it, being the newbie?'

'Ish.' She shrugged, then grinned. 'I'll win them over.'

'You always had so many mates round where we used to live,' said Tony. 'Must be hard starting again. It's different with boys. They're not as weird about friendships as girls. Like Rob. We were both newbies, new to the school at least, put on the same footie team. He's a bit of a laugh, he's got a brain so we became mates. End of story. Simple.'

Nesta nodded. 'I was the *only* new girl in our year last term. And yeah, it has been a challenge. Like everyone in our class started together in Year Seven, that's two years they've had together so the friendships have been established. And . . . it's not that anyone's been unfriendly, well except for one girl who's a right cow, Josie Riley.'

'Why's she a cow?'

Nesta wrinkled her nose. 'I bumped into her and her mates in the cloakroom when I first arrived and she put my books in the sink and turned on the taps. When I asked why she'd done that, she said, "Oh, it's an initiation for all new girls," except we both knew that I was the *only* new girl.'

'She's probably jealous, Nesta. You're great-looking and sometimes girls can't handle that. She's threatened.'

'Maybe. She was mean to me when I went to movies with Iz and Lucy – trying to humiliate us because we couldn't get in. Then some boy she was after made a beeline for me. She didn't like it. She told all of us to stick to Disney – she even said in a loud voice while looking at Lucy, "Anyone can see the midget's underage".'

'Ouch,' I said.

'Yeah. OK, so Lucy looks young but Josie didn't need to say that in front of everyone. She really annoyed me.'

'Sounds to me like she's definitely jealous of all of you. Don't let her get to you.'

'I won't, but girls like her make me realise how important it is to have the *right* mates. Mates who are on my side, who will stick up for me and me for them. Izzie and Lucy stood out straight away as solid as well as fun. I *really* want them to be my mates.'

'No one else?'

'There's a girl called TJ who seems OK but

21

she only hangs out with her mate. Izzie put out the hand to me, if you know what I mean – the hand of friendship. Izzie's really interesting. A bit mad, bit wacky, but I like that. She's into new age stuff like crystals and aromatherapy, I think she even does a bit of witchcraft.'

'What's Lucy like?'

'Lucy? Hmm. She might be small but she's got great style, like she knows how to put an outfit together. And she's funny but . . . solid too. Like you know some girls can be like hyper or giddy, the kind who scream at the slightest thing —'

'Tell me about it,' I said when, as if on cue, a bunch of girls behind us starting screaming with laughter.

'Or bitchy. Some girls can be so bitchy, but Lucy's not like that. She's, yeah, solid but, as I say, not sure she likes me.'

Tony put his hand on mine. 'Who could resist the Nesta Williams charm? She'll come round when she gets to know you better. Invite them over, put out the hand of friendship to her too. It's got to be a two-way thing. In fact, I bet she's a little intimidated. You can be scary you know.'

'Me? You think?'

'Yeah. You're stunning, you're confident —'

'But I'm not. Not all the time. I just know how to act confident.'

'Well, Lucy doesn't know that. Show her your more vulnerable side.'

'I guess I could invite her over. Her mum has said that she can decorate her bedroom so I could invite her to come and talk décor.'

'Good plan.'

And you're not going to be home when they come over to ruin it for me?'

'I am *so* not interested, except that if you want these girls as your friends, then I hope it works out. They seemed nice. But I will go out if it makes you feel better.'

'Good. Because the *last* thing I need is one of them falling for you and getting her heart broken.'

Lucy

Lucy's diary

Friday – later

Tony is the One.

Tony

Nicky? Annabelle? Janie? Jess? Marie? Bea? Or Tia?

Friday night party at Des's house. Who to take? So many girls, so little time . . .

Lucy

'Nesta's invited us over. You up for it?' asked Izzie. 'Her mum has loads of interior design mags so we can think about how to do your bedroom. Lucy, you there?'

Ohmigod, oh Lordie, oh heckity doodah, I thought. *Nesta's. That means Tony might be there. What shall I wear? Will he be in? How can I make sure I don't blush this time but say something cool and interesting and witty?*

'Lucy?'

'Yeah. Yes,' I replied. 'I'm here. Um, yeah. I'm up for it. Don't think I'm doing anything.'

Tony

I got home around four and could hear that Nesta had some of her mates over. *What were their names again?* I asked myself. *Lizzie and, drat, can't remember the name of the small one who blushed. Shame, because girls like it when you remember their name and I like to impress. Ah well. I'll have to bluff it.*

The voices were coming from . . . hey, blooming cheek! It sounded as if they were in my room. I made my way down the corridor and burst in. It was so funny because the little one was in there with Nesta and she went bright red, like she'd been caught doing something really naughty.

'Just giving Lucy the tour,' said Nesta.

Lucy. Ah, that was her name.

'Only too happy to come home and find

pretty girls in my bedroom. Hi, Lucy.'

She went even redder than before. Result! 'Hi,' she replied.

'So how's the search for the mystery man going?' I asked. 'The one with the hair?'

She shuffled about awkwardly and looked at the carpet. 'Er . . . haven't seen him again,' she muttered. She really was painfully shy.

'We need a plan,' said Nesta. 'To get Lucy noticed. You like girls, Tone. What do you look for? What do you find attractive?'

I decided to give Lucy the benefit of some good advice. She was sweet. I'd like to help her find her mystery boy. I gave her my full attention and most charming smile. 'I like girls who are funny. Who make me laugh. And girls who know who they are, what they want and where they're going. Confidence, I suppose. It's a real turn on for boys.'

For some reason, Lucy looked horrified. I even thought for a second that she was going to cry.

'Um, yes, fine,' she stuttered. 'Where's the loo, Nesta?'

Lucy

Lucy's diary

Saturday

A total nightmare of a day. I asked Izzie if she fancied Tony. She says she doesn't. Said he's too pretty. Then she asked me if I did. No way, I said, lying.

I went to Nesta's for the first time. She lives in Highgate in a fab garden flat which is so glam with lots of Eastern rugs and rich colours. Fabbie dabbie. Nesta gave me the tour while Izzie sat and read magazines. Tony arrived back and found Nesta and me in his bedroom. It felt weird being in his room looking at his private things and seeing where he sleeps. I was sooooo embarrassed that he would think I was sneaking about in his stuff like some saddo.

He must never ever ever ever find out that he is my MC, otherwise he will think I am desperate and a stalker, but I wonder if it's too late and he already knows – like, he asked if I had seen the mystery boy again and then he gave me a knowing look. Then Nesta asked what Tony wanted in a girl and he blabbed on about confidence and girls that make him laugh, all the time with this big grin on his face and a twinkle in his eye. I swear he was mocking me.

He went out again and then Nesta and Izzie spent the rest of the afternoon going on about how I could get noticed by boys. All I wanted to do was get home and hide under my duvet. I am going to give up on boys. I will never get one. I will never get one like Tony. I think he thinks I am stupid. I am a sad failure, plus I'm not even five foot tall and I have no boobs. Life stinks.

Tony

Nesta's got her mates over again, I thought as I let myself in and heard girls' voices. It was a week since I'd caught Nesta giving Lucy the tour of my room, and, happily for Nesta, she did seem to be getting well in with them. I was glad for her.

I closed the front door quietly and tiptoed over to the door to listen in on their conversation. I wasn't going to go in because I'd promised Nesta that I wouldn't get in the way of her making friends with them. They were talking about snogging. Irresistible not to stay and listen. One of them was talking about snogging a boy who tasted of onions. She hadn't been impressed. Yeah. Quite right. Big mistake. On my list of rules for snogging, fresh breath is a big must. Nesta admitted to snogging seven boys. Wow. *Way to go, sis,* I thought. I knew she'd kissed at least four. I made a mental

30

note to get her to confess all another time.

'How many have you snogged?' I heard Nesta ask. I peeked through the crack of the door to see who she'd asked. She had directed the question to the small one. Lucy. Sweet. She went red.

'None,' she said. 'I've never seen anyone I like.'

'Except mystery boy,' said the dark-haired girl, Izzie. 'Don't forget him.'

Hmm, I wonder who this mystery boy is? I asked myself. *I'm bound to know him if he's at our school.* Izzie had just begun talking about the boys she'd snogged when I had an idea. I opened the door and stood there, hands on hips, tadah! There was that look of horror on Lucy's face again, like when I caught her in my bedroom. I went over and flopped down next to her.

'The art of kissing,' I said. 'My speciality.'

'You wish,' said Nesta. 'You know nothing.'

'I know more than you think, actually,' I said, turning to Lucy. 'Want me to show you how it's done?'

'Tony,' said Nesta in a warning tone.

Little Lucy turned from pink to red to purple. I wished I had a camera.

'Leave her alone,' said Izzie.

'I was just offering to show her how it's done,' I said. 'Then she'll have something to measure it against in the future.'

Lucy giggled.

'Yeah, she'll know what it's like to be kissed by a bigheaded show-off —' Nesta started. 'Go away, Tony.'

I turned to Izzie. 'You want to try?' I asked.

'In your dreams,' she replied. Cheek. She's not my type, so why did I bother wasting the charm on her? *Save it for the ones who respond,* I thought as I turned back to the blusher by my side.

'Lucy. Do you want to learn from the Master?' I asked.

'The Master?' Nesta guffawed.

OK, I'll show you girls, I thought. I turned to look at Lucy who looked like she had frozen. I tucked a strand of hair behind her ear, tilted her face up to look at mine. Slowly, slowly does it. No rush, and actually she has a nice face, elfin with pretty blue eyes and a sweet mouth, like a pink flower, and she didn't seem to be objecting now that we were close – in fact, I could see her leaning towards me slightly. She smelled nice too, clean, of apples or some other fruit. I looked deep into her eyes. She looked back and for a second there was a flutter of chemistry. All the better . . .

'Tony!' I heard Nesta say again behind me.

Ha ha. Too late. 'Close your eyes,' I whispered to Lucy. She did as she was told. And then I kissed her. Slow, tender and, actually, nice. Better than I expected and . . . yeah, no doubt about it, she was kissing me back. Very nice. The Master rides again.

Suddenly a hand grabbed the back of my shirt.

'In the kitchen. Now!' Nesta demanded.

I laughed and got up to follow her. Before I went in, I turned back to Lucy. She looked slightly dazed but happy enough, so what was Nesta's problem? I shrugged and gave Lucy a 'What can I do?' look. She shrugged and grinned back. I was beginning to like her. She clearly had a naughty streak.

Hah! I thought as Nesta hauled me into the kitchen. *I don't care what you have to say. Your mate fancies me. I can tell. And I bet that now she's snogged me, that mystery boy she likes will take second place in line behind MOI.*

Lucy

Lucy's diary

Saturday

Arrrrghhhhhhhh! What is going on? How can life be so good and then so totally crapola? All in the same day? Same hour?

I had my first snog with Tony. OK, so he was messing about, pretending that he was the Master Snogger and offering to show how it was done but when we kissed, it was amazing. I know he felt it too. He must have done. Izzie is always saying that chemistry is a two-way thing and there was definitely some heat when we kissed, hot hot hot, and when he looked into my eyes, oo er, it was meltdown. But then afterwards, I overheard Nesta talking to him in the hall and telling him to stay away from me. Stay away from me? My heart sank. Why did she say that? That's the last thing that I wanted. I really didn't want him to stay away from me. I was happy for him to kiss me and hoped that he would do it again. And again. Very soon. There was only one thing for it. I decided that as soon as Nesta, Izzie and I were on our own, I'd tell them that Tony was my Mystery Contestant and that I wanted to be kissed by him.

Yeah right, haha Lucy Lovering, just shows what a fool you are. How could I have been so stupid as to think that I stood a chance with him? One kiss and I thought we'd be an item. I have been so naïve. Any stupid hopes I had were soon dashed because a girl showed up. Not only was she older than me, and taller than me, she was one of the prettiest girls I have ever seen, curvy with long auburn hair. She saw me in the hall when she came in. She kissed Tony then glared at me over his shoulder as if to say, keep away. He turned and spotted me. I took a step back and he did a little shrug as the girl followed him down the hall into his bedroom.

'Homework,' he said with a cheeky grin before he opened the door and disappeared. I felt like someone had put a knife in me. I was so jealous thinking of their 'homework' and him kissing her instead of me. It really hurt.

Nesta said that she is his new girlfriend. Jessica. New, old, I don't care. Who am I kidding? I do care. I care more than anything. Later Nesta and Izzie started talking about Tony and how no one in their right mind would fancy him because he's so full of himself. Seems like I will never be able to reveal that Tony is the One, my mystery boy, the love of my life.

Tony

'So is it serious with Jess, then?' asked Rob. We were in the Sixth Form recreation room sharing a cheese and tomato sarnie on our lunch break.

I shrugged. 'Dunno. You know me, mate. I'll see how it goes. How you getting on with Hannah?'

''kay.'

'Snogged her yet?'

I swear Rob blushed. 'Early days. Didn't want to push my luck.'

'Rob, my man, there's a time to be cool, there's a time to step forward. Don't delay the moment or else it might become awkward.'

Rob nodded. 'Yeah. I was going to do it. Then I wasn't sure she wanted me too.'

I sighed. 'You got to read the signals. Did she lean forward at any time?'

Rob nodded.

'Did she play with her hair, put her hand up to her throat?' I acted out the motions I'd seen girls do a thousand times when they were being coy.

'Yeah. Think so.'

'She wanted you to snog her then,' I said.

'Yeah. I was going to ask her to make sure —'

'Ask her? No. NOOO. *Never* ask a girl if you can kiss her. No. No. They want you to take command. They want you to be a gentleman but they also want you to take charge and, when it comes to kissing, it's not the time to be polite. You have to make them feel like you've been overcome with passion. You can't help yourself. You can't resist.'

Rob laughed. 'What, like, over here, you saucy wench, pucker up.'

I laughed. 'Not exactly. I despair. Rob, you're on your own from now on. And as for Hannah, well, I'll keep my fingers crossed that she takes pity on you.'

Rob chucked the rest of his sarnie at me.

Lucy

Lucy's diary

Tuesday

Can't stop thinking about Tony and when he kissed me. Was so upset that he has a girlfriend but then Nesta says they rarely last long. Decided that when the going gets tough, the tough need an image overhaul. I've read it in so many mags – that a new image can boost your confidence. So I have decided to change my image and have booked to have my hair cut after school on Thursday.

I am beginning to like Nesta. She's a good laugh and I can see that she's making a real effort to be mates with me as well as Izzie. Not sure whether I can totally trust her with my secret about Tony though. Anyway, I decided to be friendly and made her a halter top. It looks great on her and she was well chuffed.

<u>Things right with my life:</u>

Not a lot but gonna make some changes.

<u>Things wrong and need changing:</u>

I look twelve.

I am a midget. Josie Riley was right.

I am flat-chested but Iz says there are bras even for girls like me with pimples instead of nipples.

I have never had a proper boyfriend and the only boy I like has a gorgeous girl.

Everyone but me knows what they want to do later in life. I don't know who I am, what I want to do or be when I leave school.

Am going to be positive though. Make the changes. Watch out world.

Thursday

Arghhhhhhhhhhhhhhh. God, I am soooooooooooooo unhappy. Life is so unfair. I am never ever going out again or at least not for another year at least. My haircut was a major, and I mean *MAJOR*, disaster. Some idiot botched my hair and my new image is now that of a bald chicken with a few wisps on top. Not a good look. All my family stared at me when I got home – even the dogs looked freaked when they saw me. Tony will never fancy me now. Nesta and Izzie took me shopping to get a Wonderbra after my haircut from hell. Not one fitted. Not even the tiniest. I looked like a five-year-old in her mum's bra. I ran out of the Mall and went home. Had a good cry for half an hour. And now I am going to cry again . . .

Later

Have done with crying for now because it was giving me a headache. But now I have a swollen face and red eyes as well. And I still have no boobs. Iz and Nesta barged round and gave me an inflatable bra to cheer me up. It was quite funny for a nano-second until I caught sight of my hair in the mirror. I will tell Mum and Dad that I have terrible stomach ache because I really can't ever ever go out again. I have never been so miserable in my whole life.

Still can't stop thinking about Tony. I wonder if he might like a bald girlfriend, just for a change? I wonder if he ever thinks about me and that kiss? It was special, I'm sure it was. Surely he felt it? Although he may well have forgotten about me by the time I face the outside world again, because it will take about a million years to grow my hair back to a point that I can go out without scaring the neighbours.

I am so ugly.

Tony

On the way out of school on Friday night, my mobile bleeped that I had another text. I opened it up and glanced at the message. *Why haven't you called? MSSng U.* It was the fifth from Jess that afternoon. All week she'd been calling or texting, asking what I was doing, where I was going, who I was with. Alarm bells were beginning to ring. I had intended to go and see a movie with her that evening but I was beginning to feel suffocated. I don't like girls checking up on me. I headed home instead, thinking that maybe Nesta's mates would be over and I could see if I could make the cute one blush again. *Yeah, that's what I'll do*, I thought. *And sorry Jess, but you and I are history.*

Lucy

To do list:
    Make Tony fall in love with me.
    Grow a foot taller.
    Redecorate bedroom.
    Get hair fixed.

Tony

To do list:
    Clean football boots.
    Do science homework.
    Tease Nesta's mates.

Lucy

I closed my eyes and prayed that it would be OK as Betty snipped at my hair. I was over at Nesta's.

'Don't worry, Lucy,' said Izzie. 'Least she can't make it worse.'

'Understatement,' I muttered. *Please don't let Tony walk in while I'm having my hair cut,* I added to my prayer. Nesta insisted that I come over when she saw how upset I was about my hair and had talked me into letting Betty, their family hairdresser, try and fix it. I agreed in the end because I knew I couldn't go around looking like a mad person and Mum and Dad hadn't bought the 'I have a terrible stomach ache and can't go out for ten years' excuse for a second.

Betty snipped away and the girls made various encouraging noises but I kept my eyes tight shut until it was all over, cut and blow dried.

'Open your eyes now,' said Nesta.

I finally did.

'Wow,' I said. It looked fanbloomintastic. Even I had to admit it. Spiky and short at the front, and she'd even run some white blond highlights through the top. It really suited me.

'You look gorgeous,' said Izzie. 'It shows off your cheekbones.'

I changed my prayer to, *Please God, let Tony walk in now and see me looking so good.* God wasn't listening however because he didn't show. Or maybe he *was* listening and had answered my first prayer to keep Tony away and maybe you only get one prayer answered a day.

For the rest of the evening, we did each other's nails and then flicked through Nesta's mum's interior magazines. I felt so great about everything. I had a new look and soon I'd have a new room to match. And Nesta had been so fab, I was beginning to think that we really could be friends after all and that three wasn't a crowd — three was one more person to share the good times with.

'Nesta,' I asked.

'Yeah . . .'

'Um, you know Tony?'

'Yes.'

'Why doesn't he live with his mum?'

Nesta went quiet. 'She died,' she said after a few moments. 'A road accident when Tony was six months old. A year later, his dad met my mum and so my mum's the only one he's ever really known.'

'Where is he tonight?'

'Some class after school, I expect,' said Nesta.

I shot a look at Izzie. It seemed so obvious to me that Tony was the boy I'd seen and I was amazed that she hadn't put two and two together yet.

She must have finally read my mind because suddenly she clapped her hand over her mouth. 'Ohmigod,' she said. 'OhmiGOD!'

'What?' chorused Nesta and I.

'Tony,' said Izzie. '*Tony*.'

She knew. I *knew* she knew. I went scarlet. She clocked my blushing cheeks and then I knew that she *definitely* knew.

'What?' asked Nesta.

Izzie looked at me as if to say, it's your call. I decided that I would take a risk and trust Nesta.

'Tony,' I said.

46

'I know,' she said. 'What about him?'

I nodded at Izzie as if to say, feel free to say what you want. We sometimes had a telepathic thing and she got what I wasn't saying immediately.

'A boy that we didn't see in Highgate because he stays late for classes after school?' said Izzie as she waited for the penny to drop.

Nesta thumped her forehead. 'Oh. Ohhhh! Except we *did* see him! Obvious! Tony is the MC!'

I nodded.

Nesta did a small shriek.

'And he made you kiss him,' giggled Izzie.

'I really didn't mind,' I said.

'And I told him to stay away from you,' said Nesta. 'You must have hated me.'

'Not as much as I hated that red-haired girl. Jezebel.'

'Why didn't you say, Lucy?' asked Nesta.

'I was afraid you'd tell him and I'd look like such a saddo.'

At that second, we heard someone in the hall. Moments later, Tony appeared.

Tony

As I put my key in the front door and went into the hall, I could hear that Nesta's mates were round again. I followed the voices into our living room where they were lounging about on the sofas. The little one, Lucy, looked as if she'd had her hair cut. She looked good, like a cheeky cherub. She blushed when she saw me.

'Hi everyone,' I said and turned to Lucy. 'You look great.' I went and sat next to her. 'Want another kissing lesson?'

Lucy looked at the floor and then at Nesta and then at Izzie.

Nesta looked at Izzie.

Izzie looked at me.

Nesta looked at me.

Lucy looked up at the girls, glanced at me, looked at the floor again. They all looked very shifty, like I'd caught them doing something that they shouldn't be doing. And Nesta wasn't hauling me away from her mate as I expected. She and Izzie were staring at me like I had egg on my face. I checked my flies. No, they were done up, so what was going on?

'What?' I asked. 'Why are you staring?'

Lucy starting giggling and soon Izzie joined in and then Nesta. Maybe I had a chocolate moustache from the cappuccino I had on the way home in Costa. Jeez, that would be embarrassing. *Better go and check in the mirror,* I told myself. I got up to go into the hall. The girls were near to hysterical, shoulders shaking, Nesta even had tears of laughter in her eyes. Whatever they were laughing at, I couldn't see it, and I think it's mean to exclude people when you're having a good joke.

'Girls,' I said. 'Sometimes you can be *really* juvenile.'

'I thought you liked girls with a sense of humour,' Lucy was saying as I shut the door behind me.

Hmm, she's not as shy as I thought she was, I told myself.

'Not when it's directed at him,' I heard Nesta say. I put my ear to the door. 'And I won't say anything about, you know,' I strained to hear, 'about him being the MC, if you don't want.'

MC. MC what did she mean? I wondered. Then I twigged. *MC. Mystery Contestant. That's what they called the boy Lucy fancies. Hey! Wait a minute. So that was it! Blimey. I am the boy she fancies. It's me.* I put my ear back to the door. *Pff. I should have realised. It was obvious really. Best-looking boy in the school. That's me, and not because I'm vain – loads of girls have said I am.*

'Thanks,' Lucy said behind the door. 'I don't want.'

Well, well! I thought. *Don't worry, Lucy, your secret is safe with me. Hah! No wonder she had that naughty look on her face after I'd kissed her. She was probably thinking she was the only one who knew her secret. Well, she was then. But now we all know. Except . . . yeah, no one knows that I know. No one knows that it's my secret too. Hah! That will be my secret.*

'Anyway,' said Izzie. 'I reckon you could get anyone you want looking the way you do now. Play the field for a while.'

'Ah, but I have been kissed by the Master,' said Lucy, giggling again.

Yeah, you have, my little munchkin, I thought. *And don't you forget it. So I am the MC. I swear to myself that I will never let on that I know the secret but . . . that doesn't mean I can't have some fun with it.* I went to my room to call Jess and think over this latest round of developments. As Rob would say, another one bites the dust.

Lucy

'I *love* your outfit,' said Nesta when we met up outside the hall ready to go into the Clothes Show Live.

'Thanks,' I said. We had all agreed to make an effort for the event and I was pleased with what I was wearing because I had made it myself. A grey crepe wrap-over skirt and a halter-neck made from pale blue sari material left over from my room redecoration. Nesta was wearing black leather trousers, the red halter-top I had made her and a little jacket, and Izzie had on a hippie dippie outfit in purple with some great amethyst jewellery. I reckoned we looked the business.

Inside, the hall was heaving and, after we'd paid our entrance fee, we launched ourselves straight in and had a fab time cruising around the stalls, trying clothes on, and Nesta was even stopped by a model scout who gave her a card and asked her to get in touch.

As we left one stall, I noticed a group of girls from our school surrounding a boy. I could see that he was lapping up the attention and for a moment, I felt a stab of jealousy. It was Tony. Worse still, one of the girls was Josie Riley. She was flicking her hair, looking deeply into his eyes, doing all the flirty-gerty stuff. Nesta must have noticed my face fall. She linked arms.

'Don't worry, Lucy. He may be a flirt but he's not stupid.'

I wasn't so sure. He'd said that he liked confident girls and Josie was certainly that. But watching him made me think. *He must have girls swarming around him like that all the time. Well, I'm not going to be one of them.* Watching him lapping up the attention gave me a big lesson in love. *I am not going to fall at his feet like the others,* I decided. *I may still love him but I am going to be oh, so cool.*

Suddenly Josie spotted us and gave us a false smile and a wave.

'Want to go over?' asked Nesta.

I darted behind a clothes rail. 'No way,' I said.

'I couldn't bear it if he likes her.'

'OK,' said Nesta. 'And don't worry, he hasn't seen us.'

The hours flew by as we tried on more clothes and sampled every beauty product on offer. Izzie went off to buy a toe ring and Nesta and I decided to go and watch a catwalk show. We set off in the direction of the show, turned a corner and I walked smack into Josie.

'Ah, the midget,' she said and then looked at my halter-top. 'And what have you got on? The Eastern look was out years ago.'

Her friends started laughing behind her.

'She made those clothes herself and I think she looks fantastic,' said Nesta. 'I don't suppose someone with your IQ could even sew on a button.'

It was awful. I hate it when people argue. It was good of Nesta to come to my defence but the two of them were squaring up like ready for a fight. And then Josie purposely stood on Nesta's foot. I saw Nesta wince. Josie was wearing spiky heels.

'Oi,' I started.

'Oh *sorry*,' said Josie insincerely. 'Did that hurt,

Nesta?'

'Need a hand?' asked a male voice.

We all turned. It was Tony.

'No, I'm fine,' said Josie going girlie and coy.

He brushed her aside. 'Not you,' he said and put his arm around Nesta. 'You OK?'

Josie looked shocked.

'We were just admiring Lucy's outfit,' she said and her friends started sniggering behind her.

Tony turned to me. 'Yeah. Me too,' he said and he sounded like he meant it. 'Looking good, kiddo. Come on, girls, I'll buy you a cappuccino.'

Josie clearly thought he meant her too and trooped along behind us.

Tony put one arm around Nesta and the other around me and marched us away. *Ha ha. That showed her*, I thought as she sloped off.

'I thought you liked girls who were confident,' I said.

'Do me a favour,' he said. 'I like the music turned up but not that loud, if you get my meaning.' And then he looked deeply into my eyes and I swear I heard the sound of violins fill the hall.

Hold on, there actually *were* violins . . .

The catwalk show had started at the other end of the hall – laser lights were flashing and the models began to strut their stuff down the catwalk.

'I need a drink,' said Nesta. 'Can we see the show later?'

I nodded.

Tony looked torn between staying with us and going to watch the show.

'Oh go and watch the girls. That's what you came here for,' said Nesta. 'We'll catch you later.'

Tony grinned, gave us the thumbs up and set off towards the back of the hall while Nesta and I made our way over to the nearest stall and took our places in the queue. She looked shaken and leaned against a wall.

'You OK?' I asked.

She reached down and rubbed her foot. 'That really hurt,' she said. 'I didn't want to say how much. Tony can be very protective of me – if he knew that she was the girl who made my life so miserable when I first arrived at school, he might have really given her a hard time'

'What do you mean?' I asked.

'Oh, she pushed me about one day in the

cloakrooms, called me names, poured water on my books.' Nesta shrugged one shoulder as if to say it didn't matter, but I could see that just the memory of it made her eyes glisten.

I linked my arm through hers. 'Well, Josie has always been mean. I wouldn't take it personally. She's horrible to me too. Remember she calls me a midget all the time.'

Nesta nodded. 'You may be small but you're perfectly formed.'

'Exactly,' I said. 'And anyway, Nesta, you've got me and Izzie now. We'll look after you.'

Nesta's eyes filled up even more. 'Have I? Really? Because I thought you didn't like me at first.'

'I was jealous,' I admitted. 'I thought I was los-ing Izzie but I am sorry – I know now that you weren't out to steal her from me. And I'm sorry that I wasn't more welcoming. I was a cow. It can't be easy starting a new school late.'

Nesta rolled her eyes. 'Tell me about it.'

I laughed. 'Tell you about me being a cow or it being hard starting school late?'

Nesta laughed too. 'Er . . . both. Start with you

being a cow.'

In that instant, I knew that we were going to be mates, really good mates from then on. I was about to ask her more about Josie when a woman behind us tapped me on the shoulder. I turned to see what she wanted.

'Where did you get your top?' she asked.

'Oh, I made it.'

'Really? Good for you,' she said. 'I'm impressed.'

'She made this as well,' said Nesta, doing a twirl for her.

'I like doing halters,' I told her. 'They're easy to make.'

'You've got a good eye,' smiled the woman. 'A simple design but well cut. Well done.' She put her hand in her bag, produced a card and handed it to me. 'Here. Remember me when you've finished fashion college.'

'Fashion college?'

'Yes. I presume you're going to do fashion?'

It was like a light went on in my head. Ping! Of course. It was obvious. My way was clear. Fashion!

I nodded. 'Yes. I am. Course I am.'

'Well, good luck and get in touch when

you've finished. I am always looking for fresh talent and innovative design and if you carry on like this, you've got a good future in front of you.'

She saw someone she knew at the end of the coffee queue and went back to join them. Nesta took the card.

'Ohmigod,' she said.

'What?' I asked.

'That was Viv Purcell.'

The name meant nothing to me.

'*The* Viv Purcell. She's only one of hippest designers there is. Mum did a whole feature on her on the news one night last week. She is Big with a capital B.'

I felt myself glowing with pleasure. Not only had she picked me out but she was dead on – a designer, that's what I wanted to be. That is what I *was*. I could feel happiness flooding through me. I had not one, but two great mates. I had a career in front of me. I felt like doing cartwheels. In fact, if I'd been wearing trousers, I would have done!

Tony

I left the Clothes Show early and went to Rob's house to watch a movie he'd been raving about.

When I got home, I was about to go into my room when I saw Lucy coming out of the bathroom. She was beginning to grow on me and it had been fun hanging out with her, Nesta and Izzie at the show.

'Pst, Lucy,' I said. 'In here.'

She looked up and down the corridor, probably looking for my parents, but, seeing no one, she followed me into my room.

I knew she would.

I shut the door, went straight over, put her arms around my neck and kissed her. She didn't resist.

I knew she wouldn't.

'So do you want go out some time?' I asked when we came up for air. A date or two, that would be all, but she was cute, it would be fun and it was flattering to be adored the way that she clearly adored me. I was her MC. Her meestery contestant. I knew her secret.

Then, blow me down. She gave me a really slow up and down look as if she was sizing me up. Then she stuck her bottom lip out, pouted and said, 'I don't know. I'll . . . think about it.'

Holy moley and flipping heck, I thought. *Girls don't turn the Master down. What's going on?*

I gave her my killer-watt smile. 'Suit yourself,' I said. 'You're probably too young for me anyway.'

She laughed, opened the door . . . and left!

I gave her a few seconds. She'd be back. Girls always came back for more.

She didn't.

I stuck my head out into the corridor. No sign of her.

And then I laughed too. She was cool. *So . . . you want to play, do you, Lucy Lovering? I thought. OK, let game commence.*

What happens next for Lucy and Tony?
Read the *full* story in:

Mates, Dates

The Secret Story

Publication date: April 2009
ISBN: 978 1 84812 018 1
Price: £6.99

Find out more about author Cathy Hopkins
and all the books in the brilliant
Mates, Dates series at:

www.cathyhopkins.com

www.piccadillypress.co.uk

Win a shopping spree at
TOPSHOP
with £100 vouchers!

To celebrate the release of Jenny Valentine's Ten Stations we're giving away £100 of TOPSHOP vouchers to one lucky winner.

For your chance to win just answer this simple question:

Which London location is famous for its shopping?
a) Trafalgar Square
b) Oxford Street
c) Buckingham Palace

Enter online plus get other fun downloads on www.harpercollins.co.uk/jennyvalentine

Other SIGNET Books
of Special Interest

I NEVER PROMISED
YOU
A ROSE GARDEN

is the story of a sixteen-year-old girl who re-
treats from reality into the bondage of an imag-
inary kingdom. It is a beautifully written novel
that tells of her momentous struggle, aided by
a brilliant psychiatrist, to regain the real world.
It is an eloquent novel about mental illness, one
that makes a poignant plea for compassion and
understanding.

*"I'm sure it will have a good effect on lots of
people who don't realize that this sort of ex-
ploration can be done and this sort of effect
achieved."*

—KARL MENNINGER, M.D.,
THE MENNINGER FOUNDATION

Born in Brooklyn, New York, in 1932, Joanne
Greenberg was graduated from American University of Colorado and the University of London, England. She lives in a mountaintop home
in Colorado with her husband and their two
sons. Mrs. Greenberg has had four other novels
published—*The King's Persons, The Monday
Voices, In This Sign,* and *Rites of Passage*—
as well as *Summering,* a collection of short
stories.

Jenny Valentine
TEN
STATIONS

This book has been specially written and published for World Book Day 2009.

World Book Day is a worldwide celebration of books and reading, and was marked in over 30 countries around the globe last year.

For further information please see www.worldbookday.com

World Book Day in the UK and Ireland is made possible by generous sponsorship from National Book Tokens, participating publishers, authors and booksellers. Booksellers who accept the £1 World Book Day Token kindly agree to bear the full cost of redeeming it.

Jenny Valentine moved house every two years when she was growing up. She worked in a wholefood shop in Primrose Hill for fifteen years where she met many extraordinary people and sold more organic loaves than there are words in her first novel, *Finding Violet Park*. She studied English Literature at Goldsmiths College, which almost put her off reading, but not quite.

Jenny is married to a singer/songwriter and has two children. *Finding Violet Park* won the Guardian Children's Fiction Award.

Also by Jenny Valentine

Finding Violet Park
Broken Soup
The Ant Colony

Jenny Valentine

 TEN STATIONS

Lucas and his sister Mercy have good intentions
when they take their little brother Jed and
forgetful grandad Norman on a day out in
London. It's only ten stations — what could
possibly go wrong?

HarperCollins *Children's Books*

First published in Great Britain by HarperCollins *Children's Books* 2009
HarperCollins *Children's Books* is a division of
HarperCollins *Publishers* Ltd
77-85 Fulham Palace Road, Hammersmith, London, W6 8JB

www.harpercollins.co.uk

ISBN 13: 978 0 9559446 4 2

Printed and bound in Great Britain by Clays Ltd, St Ives plc

"Mum is going to kill you, Lucas Swain."

We are standing by the escalators at Leicester Square, at the bottom. I am still looking. I haven't given up yet.

Mercy says it again. "She's going to kill you."

"Why me?" I say. "Why's it only me she's going to kill? Aren't we in this together?"

My sister sniffs and shrugs and blows a green bubble out of whatever it is she's chewing. She goes almost cross-eyed, watching it before it pops. "It was *your* idea," she says. And she's right. It was.

The other morning, Mum was crashing about, slamming cupboard doors and beating packed lunches into submission, the way she does things when she wants us to know she's got too many of them to do. And I said, "Maybe we should take Jed

5

and Norman off her hands for a bit, give Mum a break, before she breaks something."

First Mercy looked at me like I was an alien. She looks at everyone like that at breakfast. Then she said, "Don't be an idiot," which is her response nine out of ten times I open my mouth. Then she finished off the first of the three bowls of Special K she was allowing herself to eat that day and glared at me and Jed while we did the parts-of-the-body word search he'd been given for homework.

When Mum finally stopped banging, Mercy stood up, rinsed out her bowl, put it on the draining board and smiled. That's when I knew she was up to something. "Mum," she said. "Why don't we take Jed and Norman off your hands for a bit and give you a break?"

Just like that. Brazen. Barefaced. Unbelievable. That's big sisters for you.

Mum tucked a strand of hair behind Mercy's ear (which Mercy *hates*) and said something about it making her day, having such a thoughtful and

mature daughter. She also said it wasn't possible.

"Why not?" Mercy said. It was half-hearted the way she said it, and you could tell she was already abandoning the idea, relieved she wasn't going to have to actually do anything.

"It's too much to ask," Mum told her. "Being in charge of a small boy and an OAP with dementia all day is harder than you'd think."

"You didn't ask," I said. "Mercy offered," and I smiled while Mercy glared at me.

Mum said it was a big responsibility. "What kind of mother would I be if I let you do that on your own?" she said.

"The kind that was getting a massage," I said. "Or eating chocolate in front of the telly."

She laughed, and you could see she was imagining herself doing just that. "So much could go wrong," she said.

I said that was true of everything. I said we could think like that about getting out of bed in the morning, but it wouldn't get us very far. As soon as

I said it, I realised that's pretty much what Mum *does* think when the alarm goes off, so I didn't push it.

"I honestly don't know if it's a good idea," she said after a minute. "Those two can be quite a handful."

Jed and Norman used to be allowed out on their own, just up to the corner shop or to the park with the dog. They were quite good at keeping an eye on each other. I don't know when they stopped doing that to everyone's satisfaction, but they did.

Mercy put her hands on her hips and said, "What kind of a handful? How hard can it be?" It's one of her talents, to grossly underestimate how hard other people try at stuff. She'll hear something on the radio, or read a book, or watch a film and say, "I could do better," without blinking, without even getting up.

I think it's what made Mum change her mind. "It's harder than you think," she said again. "Go

on then, thanks. How about next Saturday? That'd be lovely."

I remind Mercy of all that at the bottom of the escalator; the fact that it was her idea (as far as Mum was concerned), the fact that she got all the credit, the fact that she stole it. I remind her while I scan the lines of people moving around us, their backs on the way up, their faces on the way down. "She's going to kill us both," I say.

"OK! OK!" Mercy says. "So where *are* they?"

We are looking for a tall man with grey hair, and a bald patch in the middle like a fried egg. He's wearing a white shirt I think, and blue braces, and trousers from an old suit. That's what he always wears. We are looking for a boy with hair in his eyes and a red T-shirt that says **BORN 2 SK8**, even though he stays away from wheeled things if he can help it, thanks to his mild dyspraxia and a horror of scabs. We are looking for our little brother Jed and our Grandad Norman. They have taken a turning somewhere in the tunnels linking

the Piccadilly and the Northern line. They aren't behind us any more, or ahead of us, or anywhere we can see. We have lost them.

And when Mum finds out we are officially dead.

Norman moved in with us a few months ago, when Pansy died. She was my dad's mum and she was almost see-through, she was so old. One day she had a headache, the next she couldn't breathe, and then while she was in hospital with pneumonia she just sort of gave up. It only took a week.

We were all so used to Pansy being around, I don't think anyone expected her ever to die. Even on the last day, Mum was forcing custard and lasagne into her caved-in mouth, ignoring the humiliated look on her face, telling her she had to keep her strength up for when she came home. I thought about it afterwards, why any of us thought she'd go on forever, why Mum carried on feeding her and arguing with her, why we all kept saying, "See you tomorrow, Gran," and believing it. If you didn't

know Pansy, you'd take one look at her and swear she was half dead already. It was the person inside her old husk of a body that was so alive. It was the defiant light in her eyes and her terrible language and the way she laughed like she'd just heard the filthiest joke ever. That was the bit that gave up and allowed her to die. I think her body would have bitten the dust decades ago if it had the choice.

Pansy hated hospitals. She would have been livid that she died in one. Mum said it was a blessing really, because nobody wants to be old and a burden. But it wasn't a blessing for Norman because he kept forgetting she was dead, and had to be told and go through the shock of it again and again. In the end Mum gave up and told him Pansy had gone on a coach trip to Italy, and then Norman sulked because she hadn't thought to take him with her.

I suppose if anyone became a burden it was Norman because he couldn't live on his own any more, no way. He hadn't been any good at looking

after himself for a while. By the time she died, Pansy had covered their flat with signs that said TURN OFF THE GAS and YOU FED THE DOG ALREADY and STAY OUT OF THIS FRIDGE. All the tools had to be locked away because Norman would sometimes remember he used to be good at DIY and try to take the fuses out of things when they were plugged in, or take the telly apart right before *Emmerdale*.

He wouldn't have lasted five minutes on his own, so Mum took him in. She said she had to and she was right. Our house used to be his. He couldn't live on his own. It was the decent thing.

She did a lot of breathing out about it though, and general scowling. She said this was another thing that our dad had landed her with by leaving.

I said that wasn't fair because Norman wasn't as bad as all that. ("Not yet," Mum said.) He could get in and out of the shower if you showed him how to turn it on and off, and reminded him about the step. He could get dressed and everything,

pretty smartly in fact, as long as you laid out his clothes for him. It's just that you'd have to tell him when to get up or he'd stay in bed wondering where he was. And you couldn't leave him alone with a frozen chicken korma and a microwave and expect him not to be hungry when you got back. And if you left the telly on and said, "Goodnight, Grandad," you couldn't assume he'd turn it off and go to bed when he was ready. Actually you'd find him there in the morning, still dressed, his eyes all watery and bloodshot and defeated, because the man on the screen wouldn't stop talking to him and it would have been rude just to leave.

I felt bad about that.

None of that was the real Norman Swain though. That was just the bit that seemed to be taking over and getting worse. A lot of the time he was still the Grandad that I remembered and Jed enjoyed. He was brilliant at making paper aeroplanes that properly flew. Not the ones that

everyone can make, but these really complicated origami-style things that flew in circles round the sitting room and made Mercy squeal and flap her hands around like we had bats. He played the violin every morning, really *spectacularly* badly. Pansy used to hide it. But he kept practising. He'd been doing it for years, I suppose in the hope that all his hard work might one day pay off and he'd wake up and play a tune that didn't sound like a giant's nails on a blackboard. It was something to admire, that hope, even while you were lying in bed with your fingers in your ears.

The person who was most pleased about Norman moving in was Jed. They'd always got on like a house on fire, which according to Mum is funny because if you left them alone for five minutes these days that's what would happen. They've been a bit of a double-act ever since Jed was tiny. They used to hide sweet wrappers from Pansy down the back of the kitchen radiator (she found them – there were hundreds) and watch old

films together and find the same things incredibly funny. Jed never seems to notice that Norman is losing his marbles. And Norman doesn't seem to lose them so quickly around Jed. It used to be me that Jed would ask to do stuff with him, like watch Dr Who or do his glow-in-the-dark Animals of the Jungle jigsaw puzzle. Now he asks Norman.

Not that I had any time to miss my little brother's company. That was the other reason Jed was happy, because he got to share a room with me. I'm not special or anything – any one of us would have done. Jed just hates sleeping on his own. There wasn't room for Norman in the house unless somebody doubled up and there was no point in asking Mercy. Nobody even bothered. She went into this silent, thundery mood for days just in case it got mentioned.

Jed loved moving into my room. He made a big deal out of packing boxes and then unpacking them again. He acted like all his stuff had been in

storage for months and he'd forgotten what was in there and every single thing was this great surprise.

Jed's a great laugh. I've always liked him. I'm just not as into Spiderman as he is. All my books and records and posters got squeezed over to make space for his Spidey bedroom set: duvet cover, pillowcase, lampshade, *curtains* (I couldn't agree to them). So my room is not my room any more. Only half of it is. The other half belongs to Peter Parker. Mum says that's a good thing because I spent far too much time on my own in there anyway.

Norman seemed to take the whole move in his stride, like it was nothing out of the ordinary. Mum said he was "infuriatingly ungrateful". I said maybe being in his old house made him forget he'd ever been away. Maybe it was us who didn't seem grateful enough for taking up all the space and leaving him nothing more than Jed's ex-bedroom to be old in.

★

Anyway, losing a confused old man and a seven-year-old on the London Underground is a big deal and I can feel the fact of it rising in my stomach, like fear. There are so many people here and I can't see the two that we need. I keep thinking about that play where the lady says losing one parent is unfortunate, but losing both is careless. We've been doing it at college. Her voice from the black-and-white film is going round my head. It's not helping.

Mercy is just beginning to get it. She's chewing quicker and her eyes are fully open, not half shut like normal, which is either a sneer or too much stuck-together mascara, I'm never sure.

"How are we ever supposed to find them?" she's saying. "Oh my God oh my God oh my God."

Everyone behind us knows where they are going and how fast they need to get there, and we're causing a bunched up concertina-type blockage and people are getting annoyed. It's not their fault. They're commuter cattle. They can't

help it. It's like when someone throws themselves in front of a train and half the carriage thinks, "How awful" and then straightaway "How long is this going to delay me?"

I manoeuvre Mercy to a Tube map a little bit removed from the action, and at least we look like we're there for a reason and are out of the way. Mercy's eyes are brimming with water like a bath about to overflow. (We've had at least four of those since Norman moved in. The ceiling in Mum's bedroom has a new stain on it, like a giant lily pad. She said, "Maybe one day it will fall on me and put me out of my misery." I assumed she was joking and laughed.)

"I told you we shouldn't have gone on the Tube," Mercy's wailing at me. "I told you it was dangerous."

She did say that. She banged on about how she never went underground if she could help it. She said I was mad to even suggest it.

I said, "You don't go on the Tube because you

don't go anywhere. It's not exactly a lifestyle choice."

"You're not getting me on there," she said. "It's a death trap waiting to happen."

"It's ten stations," I said to her. "Camden Town to South Ken. Ten stops in between. Twenty minutes. Twenty-five."

Mercy hadn't been talking about losing people. She was just paranoid. She was on about terrorists and unattended baggage and trusting nobody and getting stuck in a tunnel forty metres below street level. She wanted to go on the bus, which I admit is way nicer because you get to see the sky and what's going on around you and everything. But the bus (or actually two buses) would take more like an hour and a half. That meant Norman would need the loo probably three times and Jed at least once, and you could guarantee it wouldn't be at the same time. Twenty minutes on the Tube meant going to the loo once at home and once at the other end, in the Science Museum, which was nothing if not good planning. Mum agreed.

In the end it was the idea of having to watch Jed and Norman pee in the street that persuaded Mercy. Nothing to do with Al-Qaeda and the axis of evil at all.

That's what I tell her. I say, "Don't give me that. You chose risking a death trap over being embarrassed without even blinking."

"God," she says. "I need a cigarette."

I remind her that smoking's not allowed on the Tube any more, since the fire at Kings Cross. I point out how disgusting it must have been when people could smoke in the trains and the stations, like one big subterranean ashtray. I remind her that it's a disgusting habit and you're not actually allowed to do it anywhere any more because everyone's finally cottoned on to how disgusting it is. I only say all this to annoy her and it works.

"Shut up," she says, and her bottom lip starts twitching and writhing, like a salted slug.

I ask her very nicely not to start crying. I can't see what use it's going to do.

"We're never going to find them," she says.

"Yes we are."

"They're going to be stuck down here forever."

I picture them giving up hope, living underground for years until Jed's all grown up and bearded and big enough to carry Norman over his shoulder, out into the light.

"Worst case scenario they'll get thrown out around midnight," I say, and I sound braver than I feel.

"Midnight?" she says. "Mum will *definitely* find out." And then she cracks and just starts yelling, "Grandad! Jed!" over and over again, at the top of her voice. I suppose I crack too, because I join in.

You'd be surprised how little attention it gets us, and what a short distance the noise we make travels. It gets swallowed up and smothered by a wall of footsteps, an ocean of muffled voices, a blanket of machine sounds. It doesn't do any good at all. After a bit I put my hand on Mercy's arm and I tell her to stop. She looks down at it, like I just found a dead

fish and put it there. But at least she stops.

I say, "Jed knows how we got here. He'll get Norman home."

"He's *seven* Lucas," she tells me. "He still believes in the tooth fairy."

"No, he doesn't," I say. "He just pretends, to make Mum happy. He told me."

Mum goes on a lot about being old. I think Jed decided to carry on believing so she wouldn't realise how old he's getting. Also, he still gets paid for his teeth, so it's not all for charity.

"They won't make it home," she says. "They'll end up at High Barnet or Heathrow or something. They'll both wet their pants."

I remind her that Mum's always talking about how she had the key to the front door when she was Jed's age, how she used to get around on the Tube by herself. I say, "Seven-year-old kids are a lot more capable than you think."

She says aren't I forgetting what happened the last time Norman and Jed went out alone, to the

chippie at the end of our road. Norman scalded himself leaning on the fish counter, and when he said he wanted to go home he meant Enfield, where he grew up. It took Jed half an hour to persuade him to walk back to our house. We heard Norman shouting in the street and had to go out and help.

"It's not being seven," she says. "It's being eighty-seven that's the problem." And for once I can't argue. A bit of public transport is one thing, but handling Norman? Even I'm not sure Jed can do that any more, and apart from him, I'm the most optimistic person in our family by a mile.

I try not to think about how badly it might be going wherever they are. I tell Mercy I don't agree with her without really meaning it, because not agreeing with her is what's expected of me, it's my job. I say, "Maybe we should just wait here for a bit longer, and they'll realise what they've done and come back."

"Maybe one of us should stay here and the other one should go and look," Mercy says. This is sensible. I am surprised.

I say, "I'll go."

"Why will you?" she says. "No, I will. I'm the oldest."

I tell her not to get lost. She gives me one of her withering looks and leaves. I'm looking at the Tube map and I'm thinking about the one we have in the kitchen, the one where the names of all the stations have been replaced by famous people from history. The Northern line is film actors and the Piccadilly line is saints, and the other lines are Italian artists and philosophers and explorers and planets and comedians. It's brilliant.

Where the lines join together, the person has got to be all of those things. So where the Jubilee and the Victoria and the Piccadilly lines meet, that's a saint and a footballer and an Italian artist, which turns out to be Gary Lineker. I know he played football in Italy years ago, but I had to

explain that one to Jed because he's only ever seen him being orange on the telly and stealing other people's crisps.

Me and Jed know that poster really well and we play this game where you have to know what all the stations are in order on any given line. I'm looking at the Tube map and I'm wondering if Jed's going to remember what the real stations are called, or if he's looking for a train to Peter Fonda, because Peter Fonda is Camden Town, and Camden town is home.

The Science Museum was Jed's choice because of this thing called the Launch Pad that's all press your own buttons and do your own tricks and climb into your own flight simulator, if you're man enough. Norman may or may not have been under the impression we were about to fly to the moon.

Mum was really worried about the whole thing. The night before she made sure me and Mercy had our phones on charge and she was charging hers

too, to give to Norman or Jed, she couldn't decide. She got two parcel labels and she wrote down their names and addresses and phone numbers, and then in the morning she tried to make them put them on. Jed thought it was funny, like he was Paddington Bear. He said could he have a hat with some marmalade sandwiches in, then he laughed at his own joke, with his arms folded across his belly.

Norman didn't like the label one bit. He kept saying he was too old to be evacuated, thank you very much, and he'd heard about these farms in Wales where the sheep were better treated than the children. He refused to have it anywhere near him. I took them both and told Mum I'd slip them in their pockets later if I got the chance. I also told her there was no need because we weren't exactly going to lose anyone. She glared at me like I wasn't funny; either that or she's psychic or something. She filled a rucksack up with sandwiches and crisps and a massive flask of tea for Norman, and

wet wipes and Savlon and plasters. She made a big deal of seeing us to the door and waving us goodbye, like we were going away for a month to trap man-eating crocodiles in the Amazon with our bare hands.

I had this image of her when we were gone, with her back against the closed front door, listening to the quiet of the house and slowly realising she had four hours off and no idea what to do with them.

"Are you sure about this?" she said to me and Mercy, and we went, "Yeah yeah, whatever, it's going to be fine."

The truth is, not one of us knew what we were in for.

The journey there was one thing. On at Peter Fonda. Norman couldn't believe the ticket machines and how swish and silver everything was. He looked bewildered, like he'd just woken up in the future, and he wouldn't let go of Jed's hand. We

had to get him through the wide luggage bit of the turnstiles because he couldn't get his ticket in and then out and then make it through the normal gates before they closed.

"God," Mercy said to me. "It's like herding cats."

The escalators were no fun either. You'd think Norman's brain went to sleep before they were invented. "Moving stairs?" he said. "I can't be doing that."

"Yes, you can, Grandad," Jed said, smiling up at him. Mercy was already on and going down, further and further away, mouthing stuff at me, miming at me to just push him.

"You just close your eyes and jump," Jed told him, and they did it, and Norman toppled a bit and then levelled out and smiled at his feet. It occurred to me that Jed knew best how to teach someone about escalators because it wasn't so long ago he'd learned himself. I wondered how old you are when you forget that kind of thing and just get on and off

like everybody else, and how old you have to be to forget that you ever knew it at all.

Norman was saying hello to people now, making Jed laugh, nodding and smiling at everyone coming the other way. He was enjoying himself. He didn't see the other end of the escalator, the sudden still bit, getting quickly closer. Mercy was standing there waiting to catch him. There were people behind me who weren't going to appreciate a pile-up.

I counted our way down. I concentrated on Norman's feet, bulky and unfamiliar in something other than slippers. As the step they were on reached ground level, I gave him a shove, just a small one. He stumbled a bit, but he didn't fall. Mercy got hold of him and stepped him aside to let other people pass.

"What did you do that for?" he said, turning on me, suddenly my elder and better again, not just someone who'd never seen an escalator before.

"Sorry, Norman," I said. "I was just trying to help."

"Norman?" he said. "Norman? It's Lance Corporal Swain to you."

I looked at Mercy and said, "Maybe we should just go home."

Jed wasn't buying that idea. He said, "You were only joking, weren't you, Grandad. You know who you are, don't you."

"Course I do," Norman said. "I'm taking my grandson here to the Science Museum. I don't need some scruffy little private trying to trip me over, that's all."

I said, "Sorry, sir. Won't happen again, sir."

He seemed happy with that.

I miss Pansy. I know she was really old and we all have to go in the end, but I still get sad that she's had her turn and now it's finished. It's a shame you only get one shot at it and I wish I believed you get more. Maybe that's why people invented reincarnation, to take the sting out of things being final. It doesn't work with Pansy though. She'd

have just thought it was a type of evaporated milk.

And anyway I'm not sure that she even minded about dying, which might be the trick about waiting till you're old to do it. By the end, she looked like she wouldn't want another minute of being alive if you paid her.

Mum thought it was best not to let Norman visit Pansy after the first time because he found it too distressing. He made a big scene, weeping on nurses' shoulders until Pansy had to take her oxygen mask off and yell at him to sit down and be quiet. I know Mum thought it was for the best, but I also know she thought Pansy would be coming home. Mum would never have planned it like that for Norman, Pansy being there one day and then disappearing the next without saying goodbye. She wouldn't have planned it because she remembers how that feels, what with my dad disappearing like he did, without a trace. She didn't mean to make Norman go through something like that. Her only hope is that he doesn't remember.

It's unnerving when Norman has flashes of total sanity. You can think you're handling a situation perfectly well, with tact and sensitivity, and then he'll say, "Good God, child. If I've got spaghetti in my moustache, just tell me!"

And his memory of the long-ago past is incredible. He can remember what his mum was wearing on his first day of school. He can picture the wallpaper and the china in their sitting room when he was a boy, the room nobody went in ever, unless they were the vicar or something. And he can remember the War like it was yesterday, because he was just old enough to fight. Sometimes I think that's the one thing he'd be happy to forget.

There are things about Norman I really like, regardless of him being in my family. Things I'd never have known if we hadn't ended up living in the same house. Like the way he can't see something written on the TV screen without reading it out loud for the benefit of the rest of us,

like, "Boston 1794" or the cast list or whatever. Mum says it's because he grew up being the only one in his family who could read. He had to tell his mum and dad what was written on signposts and posters and street corners wherever they went, until his brain just got used to saying things out loud without being asked.

Or the way he hears a joke and laughs until you think he's going to be sick, and then tells it again so he can laugh a bit more, as hard as the first time. Norman loves being happy. Or how almost any piece of classical music sends him into a state of bliss, unless it's Shostakovich, which sends him out of the room for some peace and quiet.

And how the sight of a Jack Russell – it doesn't have to be real, it can be a photo or a drawing on a place mat – will just floor him. It's the memory of his dog Jack, who died not long after Pansy and at whose funeral Norman cried more than at hers. He stood under the birch tree at the end of our garden and sobbed like his heart would break, with Jed

holding tightly on to his hand and Mercy glaring at Mum to say "I can't BELIEVE you made me be here for this".

She was looking at me like that by the time we'd managed to get Norman on to a train. We'd had to miss the first two because he refused to get on them. He was too busy reading all the posters and trying to figure out the chocolate machine, like this was the place we were taking him for the day, like the southbound Northern line platform was enough.

It was enough for Mercy. That's what I took the look to mean.

"What's Mornington Crescent?" I said to Jed as the train clattered to a stop there.

"Humphrey Bogart," he said.

Euston was Zeppo from the Marx brothers, the unfunny one whose real name was Herbert. Being the unfunny Marx brother is a bit of a bad deal, like the fifth Beatle or the third Gallagher. Nobody wants to be remembered for the things they

couldn't or didn't do. Like Henry Tandy, the British soldier who could have shot Adolf Hitler at the end of the First World War, who had him in his line of fire and spared him. Who wants to be famous for one simple act of kindness that leads directly to the death of millions of people? That's in a different league to just being the one member of the family who can't play the guitar.

Jed can't keep still on the Tube. He just doesn't see it like the rest of us do. It's not a place where you sit and read an advert for mortgages or vitamins seventeen times to avoid looking at an actual person. It's a playground, with poles to swing round and handles to dangle from and glass dividers to leave prints all over. He kept getting in people's way and getting separated from us, and he was the only one making any noise really, whooping and beeping, oblivious to the fact that everyone else was trying not to be noticed at all.

Every time the train stopped, Norman thought it was time to get off. He'd stand up and do this

thing with his trousers, sort of pinch them above the knees and straighten out the creases down the middle. I was thinking about how many times he must have done that, given that he does it every time he gets up from a chair, and how many chairs you get up from in eighty-seven years, and how in fact he might have spent two solid weeks of his life, if you add it all up, just tweaking his trousers above the knee. Maybe that's all being old amounts to, swathes of time spent doing the same thing. He did it at Warren Street ("Kirk Douglas," Jed said. "The actor with the bottom on his face.") and Goodge St ("Norman, sit down.") and Tottenham Court Road, which Jed finds easier to say than Gina Lollobrigida. When we stopped at Leicester Square where we had to change, (Northern and Piccadilly lines, Laurence Olivier, part actor part saint, see?) he didn't move and we only just got him up and out before the doors closed.

It's different moving through the Underground with someone who's older and slower than you.

People have a speed they like to go at when they're getting from A to B and it's not the speed that Norman goes. Trouble was, him and Jed weren't really noticing the queues of people behind them, like cars trying to overtake when there's traffic coming the other way. They held hands and took up the width of the narrow staircases and two thirds of our side of the corridors, and Norman was probably going as fast as he possibly could, but it wasn't fast enough. He was probably going to be worn out with the effort. It just didn't look like it. So people were tutting and braking and swearing and swerving around us. I thought Mercy was going to climb inside herself with the shame of it. Three times she said, "If I see anyone I know, I swear I'll die."

She may have wanted to ditch them or disown them on the way, but right now Mercy wants more than anything else for them to be standing here, humiliating her in public. Jed singing, Norman

blowing his nose like a bad trumpet, both of them holding signs saying WE ARE RELATED TO MERCY SWAIN. She's back from looking for them on every platform and in all the corridors. She's out of breath and red in the face from running and panicking, and three times she says there's no air down here and she can hardly breathe. She keeps asking me what we're going to do, like I've lost people on the Tube before, like I'm the expert. Three American girls have been trying to make sense of the Tube map through the backs of our heads. We need to get out of the way. I'm looking for somebody to ask. There's no one I can see who looks like it's their job to be here. Everyone is just passing through.

"What about a help point?" one of the Americans asks the others. "Let's check there."

I have no idea what a help point involves, man or machine, but I pull Mercy with me and we follow. Clearly these girls know more about what to do with a problem on the Tube than we do. They

are probably not much older than us and they have metal all over their teeth and long tanned legs and swinging hair. From behind they make me think of horses in a field. Mercy is scowling at them. She doesn't feel kind towards girls she thinks are prettier than her.

They go round the corner and back on to the platform and stop at this thing on the wall that looks like a giant loo-roll holder. They press a button and ask what the best way to Notting Hill Gate is. Notting Hill Gate is Bertrand Russell and a voice tells them to change at St Neri, I mean Holborn, and get on the Central line. I think St Neri is the patron saint of Rome and of not minding being laughed at, and I know Bertrand Russell was a philosopher, but mainly I'm looking at the white loo-roll thing and waiting for the American girls to canter away so we can use it.

There are three things you can do on the help point. Smash a red square for fire, press a green

emergency button for emergencies or try a smaller blue one for information.

"Emergency," Mercy says, reaching out to it. I stop her with my hand.

"I think we should start with information," I say.

"It's an emergency," she says, like she's speaking to someone who can't hear properly. "It's missing persons. Press the emergency button, for God's sake. Stop being so English."

I ask myself why the missing are persons instead of people, but I don't have an answer. I'm too busy picturing shutters coming down and lights flashing and alarms going off. I don't want to start a stampede over mislaying two people who both put watching Laurel and Hardy down as their best hobby.

"I'm not being English," I say. "I'm being rational. You wouldn't be familiar with it."

"Whatever, Lucas," she says. "Do it quick. They could be anywhere by now."

Once we got on the Piccadilly line train, we managed to distract Jed and Norman with biscuits. Mum put two whole packets in the rucksack – custard creams and those Garibaldi ones that Jed particularly likes because he can pick the raisins out and pretend they're dead flies. Giuseppe Garibaldi was the man who fought for twenty years in the eighteen-somethings to turn Italy into one country. It doesn't seem fair that you do all that and the only thing that gets named after you is a biscuit. He hasn't even got his own Tube station. Guglielmo Marconi has because he invented the radio, and his station is Piccadilly Circus.

I remember when I was young, way before Jed was born, when Norman and Pansy were still living in their house and Mercy was sometimes quite nice to me, and my dad was still around. We'd all be round there for Sunday lunch or something. Mum brought stuff for when we got bored, like a football and colouring books and plastic horses with hair

you could comb if you had to. Norman would walk into the front room and look at us running around and all our bags of stuff, and he'd say, "It's like Piccadilly Circus in here," every time, without fail. The other place his house looked like was Crystal Palace, when we stayed the night and forgot to switch the lights off any time we left a room.

Anyway, thanks to Garibaldi and co, they were pretty well behaved through Piccadilly Circus and Green Park (Mr Lineker), Hyde Park Corner (St Simon) and Knightsbridge, which is St Thaddeus, my favourite saint without question because he's the saint of lost causes. If you look him up online he's also the patron saint of Armenia, Florida and the Chicago Police Department, but I don't know if they realise how lame that sounds. On his website there are special prayers you can say depending on your lost cause – prayer for a drug addict, prayer for an alcoholic, prayers for marriages in difficulty and financial hardships. I can't believe that someone might really think they'd work. And at

the same time, it might be nice to think that God and all his Saints were really there, working at the prayer call-centre, that fixing whatever's broken is just a question of pressing the right button on the help point.

This is what I'm doing. I press the information button, much to Mercy's disgust, and someone asks me what I need to know. "I've lost someone," I say.

"Lost property can be located at the information desk."

"No, someone," I say. The help point line is really bad and there's a train coming in, forcing air out of the tunnel in front of it, like thunder, making it impossible to hear.

"If it was lost three days ago or more you'll have to wait a week and then go to Baker Street and fill in a form. There is a charge." I get the feeling the voice has said that before.

"It's a person!" I shout at the blue button. "*Two* persons."

"If your property has been stolen you must report it in person at a police station, yes."

"Some*one*," I say. "Not some*thing*."

The voice asks me if I'm lost. "No," I say.

I'm about to tell it that me and my sister know where we are, but we've lost my Grandad and my little brother somewhere between trains. Then Mercy starts screaming and pointing, and the train is breathing in to pull out, and there they are. We can see them, standing up at the end of a carriage, wedged between a man with two suitcases and a woman with a copy of the *Financial Times*. I don't know how we missed them on the platform. It must have been the American ponies. Jed and Norman can't have been that far away.

"Forget it," I say, and then we wave madly and shout and try to get close enough to them to bang on the window, but we can't because the train's already moving. Me and Mercy are legging it along the platform trying to keep up, trying not to run into anyone at the same time.

"Jed!" we are shouting. "GO HOME. GO STRAIGHT HOME."

He looks up at us at the last minute, just before they go into the tunnel on their way to Covent Garden and Farringdon and Kings Cross. He looks up and I can see from his face that he's only just realised we're not on the train with them. His eyes empty and he just has time to mouth back "WHAT?" and then he's gone.

"Oh. My. God." Mercy says. "Where do they think they're going?"

"I don't think they've decided," I say. "We just have to pray to St Thaddeus that they know the way home."

"Saint who?" she stares at me. "Lucas, you are such a freak."

We've got no choice but to stand there and wait for the next train. It's one of the longest three minutes I've ever counted. I can feel them getting further away from us every second.

"At least they've got their luggage labels," I say. "Someone can help them get home, or Jed

can call the number or something."

I managed to sneak the labels into both their pockets while we were in the Science Museum. Playing pickpockets and spies is something that me and Jed have done for a while. You have to plant something on the other player or take something away from them without them noticing. It's something simple at first, like a library card or a note. But then you graduate to bulkier things, Lego and satsumas and a book. Jed's better at it than me.

I'm not just saying that, I know it for sure because when I put my hand in my coat pocket to see if my phone's got signal down here, the labels are there. I can feel the eyelet laced with string before I pull them out to look, both of them, like they haven't been away.

"You're useless," Mercy says.

"Thanks," I tell her. "I appreciate it."

Jed's voice filled the tunnel at South Kensington, the one that runs under the length of Exhibition

Road. It had great acoustics. He was pretending it was the walkway to the space shuttle, saying goodbye to his family, repeating phrases like, "Clear for take off" and "Will do", adding all sorts of beeps and whirrs and rumbles. He was walking the way you see astronauts walk in films, wide legged and in slow motion, like the Michelin man but cooler. You can get to more than one museum from the tunnel. They each have their own exit. The V&A's was the best, like the entrance to a secret garden right there, no messing about. Mercy said that she'd rather have gone there, but as usual she was outnumbered and outvoted by men, whichever way she turned.

"Put a sock in it, woman," Norman barked, which worked because she clamped her mouth shut in sheer fury. "The boy wants to go into space."

"I wish he would," she said through gritted teeth. "Wish you all would."

"You don't mean that," Norman said, and you

could tell this was one of those rare instances when he's all there, inside his body, looking out.

"Don't I?" Mercy said, looking at the posters on the walls, bored.

"You don't fool me, Mercy Swain," Norman said.

Mercy looked at me then, meaning "What's the mad old bloke talking about?"

Jed said, "Grandad means he knows you're nice really so stop pretending."

Whenever I complained about Mercy, which was often, Pansy used to say that she was only vile to us because we were always there. She said that family meant much more to my sister than she'd ever let on. I could never see it myself. Usually Mercy did whatever she could to avoid us.

"She'll come round," Pansy said. "You'll be glad of each other one day." I couldn't see it happening at the time.

There was the wheel of a plane in the foyer at the Science Museum, and a clock made only of

projected light. Mercy queued up for the bag search and then waited there while I took Jed and Norman to the loo. We had to go down in a glass lift because I wasn't sure if Norman could manage any more stairs. He looked done in.

I asked him if he wanted a nice cup of tea.

He said, "Did we manage to smuggle some in then?"

I looked at Jed and wondered if he had any idea where Norman thought he was. Customs? Behind the iron curtain? A prisoner of war camp? NASA? God help us. "Yes," I said. "I hid it in my rucksack and nobody found it. You can have some when you've been."

"Righto," Norman said and he looked around the lift for the urinal. This thing was made of glass. We were visible from all sides. We didn't need Norman whipping his trousers down and peeing in the corner. Jed got the giggles.

"No Grandad," I said. "Not here! This is the lift."

"Well you'd better hurry up now I've started thinking about it," he said.

When we got back to the foyer, Mercy was fiddling with her hair and looking overjoyed and anxious at the same time. She was talking to this boy. You could tell from the look on her face, from how close they were standing, that she liked him.

"Who's that?" Jed said, pointing.

"Don't know. Keep walking."

"Why?" Jed said and Norman said, "Where's the tea?"

I took them to the café. I sat them at a table and I explained quietly to Jed that if that was someone Mercy had been trying to impress and us three had shown up like a circus act, we'd never have heard the end of it.

"It would've been funny though," Jed said.

I got Norman a cup of tea and Jed some jelly. It seemed ridiculous spending real money on food when we had the feeding of the five thousand in the rucksack a Mercy's feet. I texted her DIDN'T

Mercy came in about ten minutes later with this lunatic smile on her face. "Thanks, Lucas," she said. "You totally saved me."

We asked her who he was, me, Jed and Norman, at exactly the same time. "Oh, nobody," she said, fiddling with her hair again, grinning.

"Clearly," I said, and Norman said, "Women!"

The Launch Pad was actually really cool. Even Mercy thought so, although I reckon now she'd seen whoever it was, she'd have stayed smiling through an eight-hour opera. We photographed our own shadows and Norman spent a lot of time looking round corners and using infrared goggles and grinning. The people who worked there wore bright orange shirts and talked like kids' TV presenters, and Jed loved them. One of them did a demonstration of a bottle rocket and Jed got the job of firing it down this chute that ran the length of the ceiling. It was like he'd been selected for the Olympics.

After that we went on the flight simulators next door, but only once because any more of that could have tipped Norman over the edge. He had no idea this thing wasn't really a death-defying rollercoaster ride around the planets and I think he might have spoiled it for the others in the pod, the amount of screaming he was doing.

We had lunch where the schools eat theirs, on these steps downstairs outside the kids' loos. Mercy unpacked the rucksack and I found Norman a chair, and Jed skidded about on his knees on the polished lino, with sound effects.

"You know what?" Mercy said to me. "I'm knackered."

I said, "Mum's right – these two are a handful."

We sat together on the stairs and watched them. Norman had taken his shoes off and was rotating his brown-socked feet at the ankle, leaning back in his chair, a cheese and pickle sandwich in one hand and an apple his teeth would never manage in the other. Jed was crawling up

and down the shallow stairs on his hands and knees, clearly a predator of one kind or another, hunting his lunch, devouring his cream cheese and tomato roll without using his hands.

"It's a madhouse," Mercy said.

It felt good sitting there with her, on the same side for once, the side of sanity. I wanted to say something, mark the occasion somehow, of us not at war. "Enjoy it while it lasts," she said, smiling. "You'll do something to annoy me in a minute."

"No I won't," I said.

"Yes you will."

So I squirted apple juice at her through a straw. Mercy likes being right.

She thinks she's right now. She thinks this is a national emergency and we should be calling the National Guard. We're on the Piccadilly line train and she's ranting at me like I lost the others on purpose, like I'm acting like I don't care just because I'm staying calm. Mercy thinks that

running around like a headless chicken is the only course of action. She thinks anything less is just callous.

I think we should keep it together and get to Kings Cross (Piero della Francesca – musician, philosopher, journalist, actor, Italian artist *and* saint – quite a guy). I'm guessing those two will get off there for two reasons. One, it's how you get back on to the Northern line and then home. Two, it's where Norman always says he joined the army by getting in the wrong queue. I think he has a thing about going back to the place where he got his life so spectacularly wrong by accident. I'm trying to explain this to Mercy, but she's got no interest in what I think.

She says, "The moment my phone has a signal I am calling someone."

I say, "The moment our phones have a signal we can call Mum's mobile because one of them has got it."

"Fine," she says. "If they answer then fine. But

if they don't, it means they're still underground somewhere and I'm calling the police."

"Norman'll be glad we're worried about him," I say, "if he notices."

"Why Norman especially?" she says. "Aren't we panicking about both of them?"

"Jed knows we like him," I say. "Norman doesn't know who we are half the time."

She pulls a face at me. "Don't say things like that. They're out there on their own, remember?"

"Did you know," I say, "when Norman came back from the War, his parents had spent all his wages because they didn't expect him to survive?"

Mercy says, "You're kidding me."

I'm not. I say, "Pansy told me."

"God," she says.

"And both his brothers inherited the family business. He just worked for them."

"Did Pansy tell you that as well?"

"Yep."

"Some families are a nightmare, aren't they?"

"All families I reckon. Ours isn't exactly a picnic."

"Oh, I don't know," Mercy says. "Mum's a lot better than some of the mums I've met. And you're all right, most of the time, except when I see you of course, and Jed's got a certain appeal and... What?" She stops talking because I'm grinning at her.

"Why do you go around the whole time acting like you hate us?" I say.

"I don't."

"Yes, you do. You're horrible to everyone."

She glares at me and says, "OK, I'll stop. I'll be nice to you and Mum. I'll be nice to Jed and Norman if they ever show up. You'll get tired of it in five minutes."

I'm smiling at her and I say something about miracles and she punches me really hard in the arm, but at least she doesn't hate me. That means something.

It occurs to me that Mercy and me haven't spent this much time together *ever*.

"We see each other at meals," she says.

"Not your strong point," I tell her. Mercy hates eating. It puts her in a foul mood.

"OK," she says. "What about in the car?"

"I don't go in the car any more," I remind her. "I've got my bike."

"True."

"This is the first time in ages you and me have done anything."

"What are you saying?" she laughs.

"Nothing."

Mercy punches me again then, but I know it's because this time she's pleased with me. There's a tiny difference, if you know where to look for it. "It's not funny though, is it," she says. "We have lost them."

"I know. We are in Big Trouble."

"What do you think Mum will do?" she says after a minute.

"If she finds out?"

"When she finds out, Lucas. *When.*"

"She's going to kill you," I say, and she looks really angry with me for a second before she laughs.

"She's going to kill *us*, remember?"

"Yes," I say. "She's going to kill us."

We get to Kings Cross and we get off the train and actually I've no idea what to do next. I can't help thinking that whichever way we decide to go, they'll be where we decided not to. That they're going to get escorted home by the Transport Police and we are going to be grounded and in the doghouse forever.

"Phone her mobile then," Mercy says when we get up to street level. "Go on."

I dial and press my ear hard to the phone, and I can hardly hear it ringing because of all the noise around me. But it is ringing. That's something. It rings and rings and it goes to voice mail and the actress from *The Bill* says Mum can't take my call right now, and I'm kind of stuck about what to do.

I can't leave a message for Jed saying where the

f– are you because Mum will hear it and a) know that I swear at my little brother and b) find out that we lost him. I could leave a message for Mum, but I have no idea what to say. And if I do leave one for her and she's actually got the phone and she didn't give it to Jed or Norman, she's bound to call back and ask to speak to them.

I'm still clinging to the idea that we haven't lost yet, that she never has to know. So I hang up.

"What now?" Mercy says, and she points to a couple of fluorescent policemen in the corner of the ticket hall.

And then my phone rings. It's Mum – well, it's her mobile. I show Mercy and I pull a face and I answer it and wait to see who's calling me.

It's Jed. He actually says, "Where the f– are you?"

"What do you mean?" I laugh. "Where are you two?"

"Kings Cross," he says. "Grandad's acting like a kid."

"Where in Kings Cross?" I say, and Mercy starts looking around her, spinning in circles on the shiny floor.

"At the paper shop. He wants a bar of chocolate and I don't have any money. Can you come and get us?"

"What paper shop?" I say. "There are about a hundred."

"Across the road," Jed says, and I can hear Norman's voice and he's not sounding too happy.

"Come outside and wave," I say.

Jed says, "If Norman goes anywhere we're going to get arrested for shoplifting."

In the end I get Jed to stay on the phone and tell me how he got to the paper shop, so we can follow the route and be sure to turn up at the same one. It's small and it's divided into two by a high central shelf. We can hear Jed and Norman and see the man at the counter, who is frowning. Mercy goes one side of the middle and I go the other. They are standing at the end by the sweets.

Jed puts his arms round Mercy and hides his face in her shirt.

Norman looks at me, puts down the chocolate and says, "Where on earth did you get to? We've been worried sick."

I buy them both something and we come out of the shop and stand at the traffic lights, waiting to cross the road. Kings Cross must look like a space station to Norman. I can't begin to imagine how much it's changed since he was last here. Maybe he'd like to see it, from a place of safety of course.

I look at Mercy. "Shall we get the bus?"

She says she thought I'd never ask.

On the way home we're all a bit quiet. I think Jed's just seen a side to his Grandad he'd managed to ignore for a while. He's thoughtful, with a little frown at the top of his nose that's not normally there.

I'm thinking about what to say to Mum. I'm thinking we're going to have to tell her because it will come out somehow. You can't trust a

seven-year-old boy and a man with dementia to keep a secret.

I nudge Mercy, who's staring out of the window, and I'm about to ask her what she thinks we should do, but Norman gets there first. He's sitting at the front of the bus, his hands white-knuckled on the bar in front, like he's on a rollercoaster or something.

"I think we should keep it to ourselves," he says, and we all say, "What?"

"That you and Mercy got lost," he says. "That me and your Uncle Jed spent most of our afternoon trying to find you."

Mercy bangs her head against the window three times. Jed's laugh forces its way between his lips like a balloon deflating.

"Good idea, Norman," I say. "Let's not tell."

You can read more about Lucas and his family in
Finding Violet Park.

Look out for Jenny Valentine's
brilliant new novel

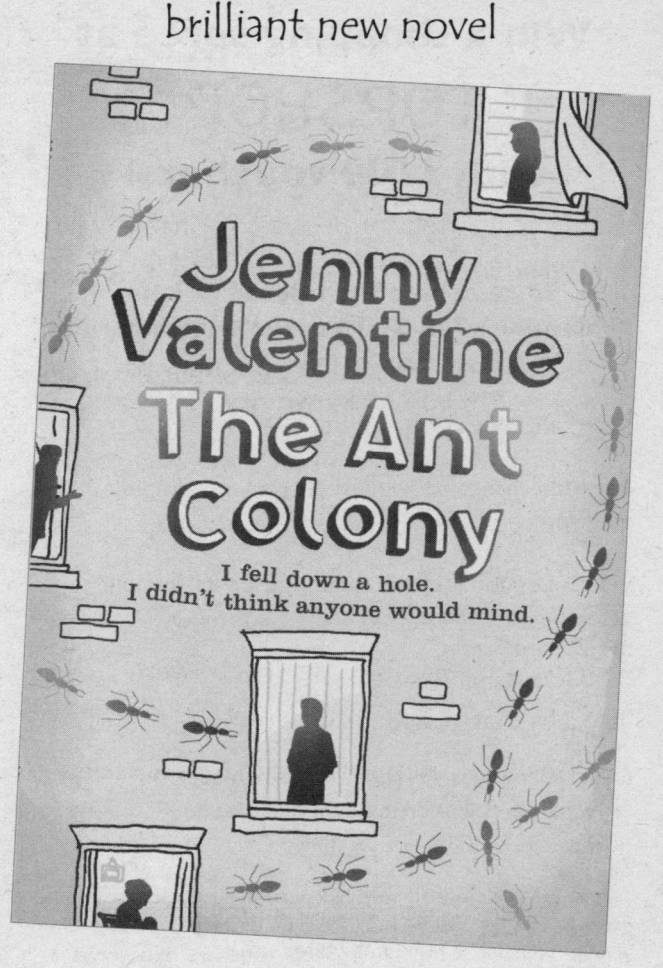

Jenny Valentine
The Ant Colony

I fell down a hole.
I didn't think anyone would mind.

In bookshops now